Josephine Rowe was born in 1984 and lives in Melbourne. Her fiction and poetry have appeared in *Meanjin*, *Overland*, *The Best Australian Stories*, *The Best Australian Poems*, *The Iowa Review*, *Griffith Review*, and *Australian Book Review*, among others, and have been reinterpreted as short films, performance pieces and broadcast on radio. Her collection of short stories *How a Moth Becomes a Boat* was published in 2010 (Hunter), and she attended the University of Iowa's International Writing Program in 2011.

TARCUTTA WAKE

stories

JOSEPHINE ROWE

UQP

First published 2012 by University of Queensland Press
PO Box 6042, St Lucia, Queensland 4067 Australia

www.uqp.com.au

Cover design by Design by Committee
Cover artwork © Josh Durham
Author illustration by John Skibinski
Typeset in 12/18pt Bembo by Post Pre-press group, Brisbane
Printed in Australia by McPherson's Printing Group

National Library of Australia cataloguing-in-publication data
is available at http://catalogue.nla.gov.au/

Tarcutta Wake / Josephine Rowe
ISBN: 978 0 7022 4930 3 (pbk)
          978 0 7022 4838 2 (pdf)
          978 0 7022 4839 9 (epub)
          978 0 7022 4840 5 (kindle)

University of Queensland Press uses papers that are natural, renewable
and recyclable products made from wood grown in sustainable forests.
The logging and manufacturing processes conform to the environmental
regulations of the country of origin.

To Patrick

Contents

—for time is the longest distance between two places.

TENNESSEE WILLIAMS

Brisbane

And she had this way of swivelling her head round, like an owl to talk to you as she drove, except not like an owl because the skin of her neck creased up in folds and she looked so old when that happened, though she wasn't, not then, and Luke would lean over and say, Watch the road, Mum.

And what I'll remember of this time is split vinyl and continental breakfasts, fights about who gets the passenger seat, a wallaby cracked over the head with the jack handle and none of us talking till Lismore even though we know she's done the right thing.

We pull in silent to the motel, a low, sandy-brick L shape, with all the doors facing onto the car park and the car park mostly empty, mostly dark. Our room is No. 17 and there is a TV that only gets two stations and one double bed which my brother and I fall into fully clothed with only our shoes kicked off. But something

1

wakes me a few hours later and I panic, forgetting where I am. I go over to the window on shaky legs and see her from the back, standing out by the road. A blonde in denim pedal pushers and white tennis shoes, standing in the light of the motel sign, like the ghost of 1967. Ghost of her younger self, holding a slim beer bottle down by her hip, fingers round its throat like she wants to swing it at something.

In the dark of the room I find the bar fridge, take a bottle of cola from inside the door. Luke lifts his head from the pillow and says, Eli, don't you drink that. Those cost like four times as much as they do in the shops, and I say, Shut up I'm not going to, and I go back to the window. Try to stand the way she does, the bottle dangling loose from my fingertips. Like I don't care if I drop it. Like I don't care about anything. She stands like that for a long time, just looking out at the road like she's waiting for someone to come pick her up.

In the morning there are flecks of rust-coloured hair dye in the bathroom sink, and Luke takes one look at her and says, That's not going to change anything, Mum, because he's older and sharper than I am but he still gets a slap for it, so we're all silent in the car again, all morning, and I wish the radio still worked.

When we get to Brisbane, she's telling us, you won't even remember. And I don't know if she's talking about Dad or the slap, or the wallaby or Victoria or that she was ever a blonde, but in any case I know she's lying, cause she's got her lips pressed into a pale line and her eyes fixed hard on the road.

The tank

It feels good to have the sun on him. To press his body into the sand, the hot wind across his bare skin finally drying out the open sores across his back, and across the backs of his arms and his legs.

He stretches his arms out ahead of him and kneads lazy fistfuls of the sand. Breathes its baked salt smell through the damp shirt, which he'd taken off and folded to lay his head on, avoiding the constellations of dried blood. He lets out a low moan. Muffled by the shirt it sounds almost sexual, but there is no one close enough to hear. The tourist season has been over for a month, the nightclub closed and the long bronze girls gone, and he had not been embarrassed to peel his clothes away from the damaged skin.

The sores appeared a day or two after he got out of the tank, and were still weeping when he came back east.

The medics didn't know what to tell him. A reaction to the chemicals and salts they used to keep the water clean, maybe. They'd never seen anything like it. He'd been told it was better not to dress them, and the fabric of the long-sleeve shirts that he wore to hide them stuck to the broken skin. Coming back, he had steeled himself for the questions. First there would be *How?* and then, almost certainly, *Why? Why would you put yourself through that? Are you fucking crazy?*

The questions would come mostly from Ella's friends. They were all like that, her friends. Quick to slag off the ADF; quicker still to scrabble for any gory morsel he might throw them. They wanted waterboarding, starvation, dogs. They wanted to tell him how barbaric it all was.

Yeah, well, he'd tell them. They're not prepping us for a crafternoon.

He'd stopped trying to explain the how and the why; they would always twist it somehow, use it against him. Use it to turn Ella against him. Ella used to call them off, change the subject. Talk about the Rilke quotes that cluttered his letters from Afghanistan. *Let everything happen to you, beauty and terror . . .* But these days she just watched to see what he'd say. To see how long it took him to stand up, drain his beer and throw her the keys to his car. Might see you back at the ranch, El, and he'd barrel home through the night air, walking beside the rail lines with his hands balled up in his pockets and the

5

sound of the freight trains humming through the tracks. He knew how they talked about him when he was out of the room. Thought he was violent, that he had to be, to have been where he'd been.

When he came back from selection she was waiting in the kitchen of his flat. He set his gear down on the floor and she stood up.

So that's it then?

That's it for now.

But you said if you failed . . .

I didn't fail, I just didn't pass. Medical release, he said, unbuttoning his shirt to show her.

My god, Laith. You let them do that to you?

It just happened. It's no one's fault. I can apply again next year.

No. I mean, yes, you can, you can do whatever you want. But I'm not going to wait for you next time.

It was his turn to say something but there wasn't anything. A freight train screamed past, and the building shuddered as though it might shake apart. He counted the shipping containers. Thought about the stories friends had told him about riding them, not caring where they were headed, strapping themselves to the ladder rails so they didn't roll off while they slept.

After Ella walked out he drove seven hours down to Rosslyn Bay, and stood waiting at the pier until the first ferry arrived.

★

His father had brought him here when he was seven or eight. The most beautiful place in the country, he'd said. You catch a glass-bottom boat across and you can ride in the boom nets. But the island wasn't the way his father remembered it. There was something pretend about the place, Laith knew, and they spent the day hiding their disappointment from each other as they moved among the throngs of sunburnt Brits. Lunch was fish and chips eaten wordlessly in the glare of white plastic furniture, the families around them squealing, scolding, his father's enthusiasm slipping into something tight-jawed and desperate. Another thing he'd planned for, saved up for, that had fallen on its face. Laith wanted to tell him it was okay, but he didn't know how. Later he'd sliced his foot open on an oyster rock while snorkelling. His father picked the pieces of shell out of the cut with a pair of borrowed tweezers, and somehow things had become easier after that. On the way back to the mainland the boat passed over a fever of stingrays, and the sight of them through the glass was enough to colour everything else and outstrip it.

It was something he'd remembered while inside the tank. Remembered or dreamed it; after the first day or so there was less and less difference between the two. He knew he'd have time to think about a lot of things inside the tank, and he'd saved them up in the months prior to selection. Someone had said it would feel like weeks in there, that blokes who'd nailed all the physical stuff – the twenty clicker and the retraining sessions – were tapping out before the end of the second day, signing their Withdrawal at Own Request forms while their hands were still wet. Laith slipped into the blood-warm water and they closed the lid on him.

The door of the tank would not be locked. They had been emphatic about that. He could climb out whenever he wanted, though he knew that would mean going home early. If he climbed out to piss, he'd be going home early. They would open the tank – this happened eight times, though he could not tell if there was any regularity to it – and when they did he would be overwhelmed by the smell of their skin and their breath. They checked his eyes and asked whether he'd had enough yet, before closing the lid on him again. They never told him how long it had been, though once they gave him water and he figured he must be halfway through.

It wasn't cold in the tank. It wasn't anything. Just black and silent, and he was alone with the aching for rest he'd had since he got there. He'd kept a mental list of things that needed sorting out. But it was his son who kept returning; a recurrence that seemed measured, as though he were walking up and down a small rise, coming in and out of view. He would be five now, nearly six. She'd called him Oscar, and some nights Laith would stay up

8

online and look through Angela's Facebook albums while Ella was sleeping. No birthday cards, Angela had told him, her arm across her swollen belly. No phone calls, nothing at all. But she hadn't hidden him away. Here were the birthday parties, the trips to the snow. The everyday snapshots with dogs and bicycles. Laith had watched him grow up from behind one-way glass.

I won't ask you for anything, ever, she said. And I won't make him hate you. But I don't want him to have what I had. What both of us had.

I didn't mind it. It didn't do me any harm.

You did. And it did.

What are you going to tell him?

I'll tell him the truth.

And the truth is?

That I thought it was for the best.

Ange . . . this is stupid. We can fix this.

She'd closed her eyes then. Other people are going to have to make up for all the wrong we've done to each other, she said, her voice steady and her palms flat against the table.

But no one had, at least not for him. No one had made up for any of it. When they finally let him out of the tank he stood naked on shaky legs and knew all of it for what it was.

The breeze coming off the ocean has cooled when he lifts himself out of the groove he has made in the sand. Every part of him still aching from the fourteen days out west. In the lodge he takes the towels from the bathroom and spreads them across the bedsheets before lying down. Just make the last thing right, his father had told him as they watched the stingrays through the glass floor of the boat. You get the last thing right, and the rest of it doesn't matter so much.

Adeline

In the middle of December the roof caved in. It had been the wettest spring for many years and everything had been quietly mouldering away up there for months. Then the sudden seam that appeared in the ceiling above my bed; the covers drenched in stale water, smattered with broken plaster. The sheets clung to my legs and a clump of sodden insulation batting lay across my chest like a dead wet cat. Everything was coated in a sticky white-grey dust. Colour of dirty goose feathers, city snow.

I should have gotten up then, walked to a safer part of the house and called the real estate to tell them what had happened, and that it hadn't been my fault. But I'd been dreaming about Adeline, and I was so sure that if I woke up properly, there'd be the news that there was nothing they could do for her, that they'd had to turn her off. So I tried to ignore the hole in the roof, to find my way back to the old house where Adeline still sits waiting on the back veranda, her dark hair knotted at the back of her neck and everything steeped in the medicinal smell of her skin.

Even here, it is raining. The backyard is cluttered with cardboard boxes going soft in the rain. Adeline takes a draw on her damp cigarette and says, Well, what do you think?

The sides of the boxes are disintegrating and things are starting to spill out, gimcracks and books, clothes with patterns that I recognise right away.

Is this everything? I ask.

It's everything, she says.

Okay then. Alright. Good.

And down in the old garage the girl we tried to share – the girl we tried to share, and could not share – is teaching you to play guitar, and the band of light that comes from beneath the door is the colour of dirty goose feathers, the colour of city snow. I go down and I bang on the door for a while but she just plucks harder at the cheap nylon strings saying, This is A, this is G, this is F, her voice like a cracked porcelain dish spilling over, This is B, this is E, and eventually I walk away.

Cotton

You could tell just by how clean her hair was, someone told the papers afterwards. You could tell she had money, that she was somebody. Had been somebody.

On the morning we found out, we didn't say very much. We smoked a lot and passed the papers around the table, comparing the stories in the tabloids with the stories in the broadsheets.

Somewhere there was a matchbox, her baby teeth nestled into cotton wool. Somewhere the bronzed baby shoes, the envelope of feathery blonde curls, kept safe.

All you really have to do is be here

Someone set fire to the place a couple of years ago, and one of the back rooms was left badly damaged. Roscoe just cleared out what was left of the furniture, swept up the shards from the petrol bomb and locked the door.

Wasn't much took place in there anyway, he told her when she started.

Who did it, do you think?

Just bored kids, probably. Nothing for them to do out here.

I suppose fire's thrilling when you're a kid.

Stays thrilling to some people, he says. You'll be okay till the end of July?

That's fine. I'm not going anywhere.

She'd seen the film when she was young, a wartime drama that had bored her to sleep on the green chevron couch. Slow, saturated yellows of the 1970s, and the kind of ending her mother cried at, though that wasn't saying much. It wasn't until she moved out here that she remembered, driving past the heaped stone wall and beyond it, the greying weatherboard farmhouse, the surrounding paddocks dotted with the hulking frames of ruined machinery. A peeling sign read *Open to visitors, Sat & Sun*, and beneath that, *Short Term Help Required*.

Roscoe was silver and wiry, the lines of his face resembling animal tracks over dusty ground. When she asked about what kind of help was required he smiled, broad and askew.

Tell you the truth, love, all you really have to do is be here. Eleven a.m. till five p.m., both days. My sister's chemo sessions start in Sydney next week, and I'm getting a bit desperate.

She followed him through the house, purpose built and furnished for the film and unchanged in the four decades since. A DVD of the film played on continuous loop on a flat screen in one corner of the living area. Everything else looked makeshift, salvaged, fashioned from packing crates and produce boxes.

Austerity measures, said Roscoe, and flipped through a stack of ration cards. Try to make sure these don't go missing. They're worth a packet these days. Ironic, eh?

He gave her a wink then, and handed her a cluster of rusty keys.

There's a folder in the top drawer of the bureau with

all the information you'll need. Names and dates. Trivia and such. You'll get the odd smartarse that just wants you to know how much they know. But if there's anyone you get a bad feeling about, you call Dave. Number's written there in the folder. Film creeps are the worst creeps, I can tell you.

On the outside wall there is still a black smoke smear climbing up from the window, the window itself covered over with a raw sheet of plywood. On slow days she'll unlock the door of the burnt-out room, where the walls and ceiling have not been repainted, and the damp charry scent of the ruined floorboards reminds her of camping in winter, of sleeping in her clothes and conversations beneath a ruined rail bridge. Some afternoons she scrapes one of the dining chairs into the room and closes the door behind her. Sits and tries to read, her hand on her belly, waiting to feel something kick. Though it's too soon. She knows that much.

All the other rooms were repainted and reopened to the public within two months of the fire, Roscoe's little laminated notices reinstated: This is where such and such happened. This is where whatsherface said or did or broke this. She comes in at 10.45 to set up the DVD and murmurs along with it while rearranging the rack of dusty souvenir postcards. *Darcy? He's over in Katoomba working on the funicular . . .*

Visitors pay five dollars to walk around the farmhouse, sliding their fingers over everything and waiting for something to happen. They pick up the ancient flipside toaster like it's magic. This is where so and so made toast, she thinks, and asks them to please not disturb anything. To please get out of the bed, the bathtub, et cetera, that they can re-enact their favourite scenes when they get home.

Jack Thompson will not be standing outside, waiting for you in the rain, she wants to tell them. No, those aren't really his pyjamas. Your life is not a movie, unless that movie is the final scene of *The Purple Rose of Cairo*.

Her own house still feels like a film set. Her own house does not yet feel like her own house, although it is. The first compensation payment went towards the deposit. In the shed she finds Golden Fleece oil cans, rusty fox traps with their terrible jaws snapped shut, a water-damaged book on barbed wire. Whoever lived here before lived here a long time, had made and grown things. But it's wild out there now. Some of the herbs and vegetables have lasted through the several months of vacancy, but most are choked by weeds or gone to seed. In the rental properties that came before there had never been any point to it, growing plants for the next tenants to eat, for them to look at or not look at, take care of or let die. Anything she grew, she grew in pots, hauling them into the back seat of the car when it was time to move on. But here, it is different. She can finish what somebody else has started, and still be here to see what comes of it.

The first few weeks have been spent ripping out the dead things, digging the garden beds over and rebricking their borders. The ground is soft with late-autumn rain and everything comes up easily in her hands. At dusk her muddy boots and bulky woollen jumpers are kicked and shrugged off just inside the back door, ready for the next afternoon. Inside the house, little has changed since the removalists brought everything in three weeks ago. Cardboard boxes still line the hallway, filled with books and clothes she can't get into. During the evenings the house has a gentle clicking to it, the sound of crustaceans underwater, and the winter lilac of the sky makes her believe that yes, she might have drowned out here. Standing in the old clawfoot tub, she runs hot water over a vial of progesterone, wipes a swab around the bruised injection site. The first few had nearly made her throw up, the feeling of the cool oil blooming from the needle. But it's easy now, mechanical.

Moonlight soaks through a second-hand sheet. Somewhere out there, a barking owl, its sound of a woman screaming. It's been a long time since she screamed. Her noises are small, involuntary. She keeps her left hand pressed against her stomach, doesn't think on anyone. There's no one to think on, and it's better like that, stronger, as though part of it dissolves when shared. When she finishes she lies back and listens to the blood pounding soft in her head. Tells herself she'll put up curtains this week, cook proper meals. She'll unpack the record player and it won't be so quiet. Nina, Dylan, The Boss. Mance Lipscomb to drown out the owls' screaming and the lonely underwater noises. Maybe she'll haul the furniture around, reassemble the bookshelves. But she's unsure about how much heavy lifting she's supposed to be doing. This was the first time in her life that she'd hired removalists, and it had felt like stupid luxury. For fifteen years she'd traded a slab of beer or a bottle of scotch for a second pair of strong arms and it had worked out fine. But the Levines didn't want her to strain anything.

Let us take care of it, they said.

Sure, she relented. Go ahead and set it up for Tuesday.

The following week a trio of men had come into her apartment with all their flannel and lifting straps, and she stood back and flapped her hands in some ineffectual choreography while they carried out her armchairs, her kitchen table, her refrigerator. She watched them put the fridge onto the truck. A few days earlier she had defrosted the freezer – it had been a solid block of ice for the best part of a year. She'd just chipped pieces off now and then when she couldn't get the door to close. Finally she unplugged it from the wall and packed the floor around it with old towels. Throughout the day things emerged from the ice; packages of peas, a half-box of waffles, an exploded beer bottle and, inexplicably, a blue toy train. She chiselled it free and ran the hot tap over it. The little rubber wheels spun as she pushed it across the draining board with her index finger, not understanding how it came to be there in the freezer. Once the ice had completely defrosted and the towels were soaked with melt-water, the smell of chemical cold, she put the toy train back inside the freezer door. Now it rattled around inside the taped fridge as the men hoisted and shuffled it to the back of the truck.

She considers telling the Levines about the freezer train when they fly in to visit her at the new house at week fourteen. There is still the question of which books to unpack, which pictures to hang. How to make herself look like the kind of person who can keep something safe. New subscriptions to *The Economist* and *Foreign Affairs* are already stacked up on the kitchen table. Bub will be politically aware, she will joke, though in reality the articles make her feel soft, blunt; she reads over the same line two or three times without taking any meaning from it. Stills from the last three ultrasounds are there with the magazines. At ten weeks, it looks like a monkey smoking a cigarette. Though if neither of them mentions the similarity, she won't draw their attention to the fact. Their child's potential monkeyness is their problem.

They are still calling it compensation, although the official sum, the one written into the contract, is much smaller than the amount she received. But they're polite. Good god, are they ever polite, so compensation it is. She could float two years on it out here, in this town where apology is so close to everybody's mouth, as if tucked just inside the lower lip. Bump into someone in the street and it just tumbles out: *I'm sorry. Excuse me, I'm sorry.*

Hell, we're all sorry, she wants to respond. We're all sorry about something, aren't we?

One night her brother calls from interstate. He doesn't like what she's doing but he doesn't have much to say about it.

Just letting you know I'm heading over to Spain next week, he tells her.

Well. Bueno.

Want anything? he asks, as though Spain is the milk bar at the end of the street.

A chocolate frog and a bag of snakes.

Ha.

No thanks, I'm all good here.

A good bottle of PX, maybe.

I'm not drinking, I told you.

Yeah. I'd stop drinking too if someone put six figures in front of me.

It isn't six figures.

You should think about telling Mum. I don't like you hiding over there on your own. You're being rabbity.

Okay, she says. I'll think about it.

Like hell you will. I could've leant you something, you know that right? If it was about the money.

It isn't about the money.

Then what? What is it about?

★

21

Standing in the burnt room, where nothing of great importance was ever filmed, where nothing has started to kick, she wants to go back through all the rooms of her life, place everything that mattered, prop up laminated notices; this is where I grew thin and breastless, where my laugh softened to a scratch; this is where god became a lowercase word; this is where I surfaced; this is where I stood, and watched, and couldn't do anything. This is where, and this is where.

Outside the house, on the other side of the plywood, somebody coughs and spits. There's the sound of the screen door opening and banging closed, a throat being cleared. A walk-in – she would have heard a car if there was one. No noise of an engine, no tyres crunching the loose stone drive.

A man stands in the centre of the room, fingers of one hand resting lightly on the rough-hewn table. He is looking up at the television, where the water tower scene is playing out. Next will come the struggle, Jenny Agutter storming down the hill, holding up the shoulder of her torn dress.

Can I help you with anything? It's supposed to be five dollars but we're closing soon.

He turns around then, and his expression is that of someone stranded several hours in a small airport. He looks at her, looks past her into the room she has just walked from.

In the mornings we would sometimes hear him singing

In the mornings we would sometimes hear him singing. His voice came strong across the greying, toothless fence, across the famous nine-foot tomato plants and the green outdoor table covered in empty bottles and cigarette ash. It got in through broken sash windows held up by encyclopaedias and cask-wine boxes, and it found all of us there, sharing the one large roof but watching the paint flake from different ceilings.

Inside we were standing at our kitchen sinks and our bathroom sinks; we were reading at desks, and at the tables that functioned as desks; we were sitting on unmade beds coaxing music from battered instruments; we were yelling at the newspaper, our hands still sticky with wallpaper glue and our mouths still sticky with sleep; we were falling in love with Rothko, finding beautiful ways to talk about violence;

we were ravenous and restless; we were so still we collected dust.

When we heard him singing we would pause with our toothbrushes in our mouths, our hands in the grey dishwater. We forgot our hunger, lifted our faces from the works of Cisneros and Stein, let the instruments sleep in our arms. We would lower our fists, we would listen.

All of us were in between, rising or falling; we wouldn't know which way till afterwards. There was so much to look forward to. There was so much to be sorry about. For that time we lived in the midst of each other's static, the murmurings of radios and televisions that came through walls, muffled conversations that rose from the floor or floated down through the ceiling. There were no true secrets. In place of secrets we kept contraband animals, a menagerie of cats and small dogs. When one of them became sick and died we buried it at the back of the block, under the tree that sheltered the red leather lounge suite somebody had dragged out there two Januarys before. In the height of summer we drank tequila and cycled to the beach to watch the waves toss jellyfish up onto the sand. We slept under wet towels, or we slathered our skins in Aerogard and stretched out on old sheets in the Alister Clark Memorial Rose Gardens, listening to the arguments Blessington Street staged with itself in the dead heat of the early hours.

In winter we watched our breath cloud the air above our beds. We bought firewood from the bent man near the railway bridge, his tattered woollen cardigan with splinters and sawdust caught in the weave. We lit fires under blocked chimneys and all our clothes smelled of smoke. Grown men fell asleep on our doorsteps, curled up like children, and we stepped around them to unlock our doors, saying *just this once* while riding high on the shoulders of our own benevolence. Working girls redid their make-up in the yellow light of our stairwells, in the brief interludes between blown or stolen bulbs. Our bicycles disappeared from the railing we chained them to and an anonymous hand scrawled *One day soon I will be waiting inside for you* above the door of No. 8.

But in the mornings we would sometimes hear him singing, and his voice thrummed through all the busted hot water systems and dirty sheets and discon-nection notices, through the discarded needles and the places where our bicycles used to be. His voice touched these things the way a small child touches the fur of an unfamiliar dog, not conceiving of the possibility of being bitten. His voice made these things better than they were, lifting them above the seedy and the broken and the dangerous so that they became something else; a bronze cast of something seedy and broken, a collo-dion photograph of something broken and dangerous. He did this without knowing it, and although we could not understand the language he sang in, we under-stood what it meant to keep your voice – if only your voice – and to use it whenever you could in an ugly apartment where you went for weeks without anyone saying your name. Where basil and coriander struggled from plastic pots along the kitchen window sill, growing in the three-hour blade of sunlight that cut between the two buildings like they were two halves of a failed cake.

Some days we saw him in the fresh produce section of the supermarket, and did not understand how such a voice came from such a man. We would feign distraction, turning away from his rum-blossomed face in our sudden desperation for artichokes, for tamarillos. Or we would exchange awkward pleasantries while he selected ripe apricots from the display and broke them open with his knotty hands. He would bite into one half of the fruit, then spit it right back out onto the green linoleum floor. Pah, he said. No good. Taste of nothing, you see. Then he would offer the other half to us for confirmation. Nothing at all, we would agree, awed by his disregard for supermarket conduct.

When the development notices arrived, addressed to The Occupant instead of to our names, some of us had already cottoned on, spooked by men with retractable tapes measuring the low brick wall that housed our letterboxes, and which the working girls would sit along in a fleshy row, like birds or cats or cabs, when business was bad and their feet had started to ache. Some of us had already started packing. Some of us knew the signs.

We are gone now, all of us. And the corner stores are clothing stores, and the arts supply is closed. The pubs where we shot pool and slouch-danced to Red Right Hand on the jukebox, those pubs do not have pool tables or jukeboxes anymore.

In the mornings I get up, I make coffee, the cat asks to be fed. I share no walls, no roof, no backyard. I can go naked into the backyard if I want to, and I do sometimes, to remind myself I can. The only radio I hear is my own, reiterating the small issues in the hope they will distract from the real issues. And yes, people still sing – there will always be singing – but it's never the kind that makes something better than it is. My disconnection notices are just disconnection notices. My dirty sheets, they're just that.

The taxidermist's wife

The Museum of Taxidermy was nothing like the natural history section of the State Museum. The bear at the MOT had a shiny coat and its glass eyes looked like real bear eyes. The fur was not coming off the viscacha in tufts, all the zebra's stripes matched up and you couldn't see the lions' seams. None of the animals were in glass cabinets; none of them had hundred-year-old paper tags with serial numbers and Latin names in spidery handwriting.

The MOT had been built as a theatre in the twenties. The stage was still there, with its red velvet curtains pulled aside. Some of the animals stood on the stage awkwardly, as if in the middle of a dress rehearsal where everyone had forgotten their lines. The animals that were not on the stage – the audience animals – were waiting patiently for the actor animals to remember.

The taxidermist lived with his wife in a small house behind the theatre–museum. They'd set up a lounge room in what had once been a dressing room. The wife was in there most days, sitting on the worn-out leather couch and watching daytime television or reading southern gothic novels, while the taxidermist took care of the business and made sure that visitors paid the two dollar entry.

It was the taxidermist's wife who fascinated us more than anything, more than the stiff animals or the display of taxidermy tools that looked like instruments of meticulous torture. The taxidermist's wife, who was in love with a man devoted to preserving the dead. For a time we liked to speculate about who her former lovers might be – the Latin professor, the obituarist, the forensics photographer. But the taxidermist's wife walked right through the walls of the ideas we had for her, back to the faded couch and Carson McCullers.

She knew almost nothing about the taxidermy process, and could not answer any of our questions, redirecting us to her husband when we asked about ear pliers or polyurethane forms.

But she understood the gentleness of such work. She knew a thing or two about responsibility. If we came in early on a Thursday, we'd find her kneeling in front of the pet cabinet with a small white box open on her lap. The pet cabinet was a cupboard stacked with dozens of small white boxes, and in each was the preserved skin of a cat or a small dog, or in one case, a large coffee-coloured rabbit.

Nobody was coming back for any of them. Loving owners had grieved for them years ago when they died of old age or snail pellets or traffic, and they were brought to the taxidermist wrapped in towels or soft cloth. But these animals were to remain eyeless, jawless, shapeless, marking the point where that grief was no longer a thousand-dollar grief or a twelve-hundred-and fifty-dollar grief.

Once a week, the taxidermist's wife would take each skin and rearrange it in its box so that it wouldn't develop unnatural creases. There was a reverence to it, the way she tucked their tails and paws in. Sometimes we'd hear her speaking softly to the skins, You were so beautiful. Who'd ever wanna get over you, hey? Who'd ever wanna leave you behind?

Vending machine at the end of the world

He moved into a hotel that had my name and called most nights from the payphone in the hallway. Before that he used to call from a phone box on the corner of Second Avenue and Pine, and I could always hear sirens in the background, and drunks shouting at each other. *Fuck you motherfuckers, I can fly.* That was when he was sleeping in a park at night, and working during the day selling tickets over the phone for the Seattle Opera. The money he earned selling opera tickets he spent on beer and international phone cards. Then he cut down on beer and moved into the hotel that had my name. That kind of love scared the hell out of me. The kind of love that makes a person cut down on beer and move into a hotel just because of its name.

When he called it was nearly midnight for me but early morning for him. I lay on my stomach on the ugly grey carpet of the house that I grew up in, the phone cord stretched to the front door so I could blow cigarette smoke through the wire screen. I imagined him sitting with his face to the wall, ignoring the other residents as they tramped along the hallway. I imagined he still looked a little homeless. JFK once stayed here, he told me. Elvis stayed here. But now the cage elevators were breaking down twice, three times a week and it was fourteen flights of stairs to the room that housed his unrefrigerated forties and his stolen desk.

His two favourite topics of conversation were the Lesser Prairie Chicken, and a vending machine in Fremont that stood alone in the middle of a vacant block. The vending machine had an unlabelled mystery button underneath all of the labelled buttons for the usual drinks. He liked to speculate about what kind of soda would be dispensed if he were to push the mystery button. Would it be Tab or would it be Mr. Pibb? He rattled off a list of dead cola brands from his childhood, most of which I didn't recognise because his childhood was eleven years earlier than mine, and on the other side of the world.

I bet it's Tab, he finally said. He had turned the vending machine into a time travelling device. He wanted a Tab summer. He wanted it to be 1982 in Atlanta, Georgia, before the methadone trips to Mexico and the minor prison stints for DUI. He wanted to be on his uncle's farm, raising Lesser Prairie Chickens. He wanted to be anywhere but Seattle, selling tickets for the opera.

One night he called and told me he'd gone to Fremont. He'd pushed the mystery button on the vending machine at the end of the world.

And you know what I got?

What'd you get? I asked.

Fucking Sprite.

And Atlanta, Georgia in 1982 was bleached out and unreachable and he and I had one less thing to talk about.

Dixieland

Friday night in a West Australian basement, and the six-man jazz band is playing Do You Know What It Means To Miss New Orleans to sixty people who entered through a red phone box, ready to drink and dance like they were other people, and it was a different time and place. All the heat of the day is trapped in that room, and the place smells like sweat and brass. When the band introduce the numbers their accents are broad Australian, but when they sing it's pure Dixieland.

The elderly doorman is dancing slow swing with a young woman in a sequinned dress. Then the girl in the polka-dot dress, and the girl in the red lace dress. He switches girls after every song. All the girls are big-calved and soft-looking, and he moves them around the old floorboards with a sad grace.

He still wears his wedding ring, and when the band plays Sweet Lorraine he stops dancing. He always sits out for Sweet Lorraine, and watches the band from a small table which he and his wife donated to the club in the eighties. The table once contained an antique sewing machine, but the sewing machine is gone and all that remains is the cast-iron foot pedal, and an iron wheel which is beautiful and useless. He presses the foot pedal in time with the music and the wheel spins around but it isn't connected to anything. Sometimes he opens and closes the small drawers at the sides of the table, but there is nothing in the drawers now except for bottle caps and ticket stubs from the weekly raffle.

When Sweet Lorraine is over he stands again and goes back to the dance floor to dance with Lana, who is twenty-three and moves with the same elegant sadness. The elegance is something she picked up recently, but she was born with that sadness. They dance together for Louisiana Fairytale and Mack the Knife. They go wild for Tiger Rag. When Lana comes back to your table she is flushed and breathless. She laughs and kicks off her cork wedge sandals and you wish you could take her to Miami, drag her into the early retirement you always threaten when she wears those tacky shoes. You wish you could take her anywhere, that she'd let you make her happy.

The old tin signs on the walls advertise cigarettes and fountain pens that have been out of production for decades, and chewing gum and soft drinks that Australia got a taste for in the forties when the Yanks swept through with easy money and Coca-Cola. You're there in your plaid Texan shirt. Your best friend in her Florida retirement heels. Everyone in the low-ceilinged room dreaming America.

Belonging to Sonja

There are bloodstains on the mattress. Old bloodstains, dried to the colour of rust. She notices them when she strips the sheets off his bed for the first time. Kate stands at the end of the bed with the sheet in her hand. She knows the percentage of used mattresses in the world that do not have bloodstains must be a very small percentage. Still. One more thing belonging to Sonja, in a long list of things belonging to Sonja. Medication. Books. A winter coat. All the little traces of her in the bathroom cabinet; tampons, razors. All the little traces she left on him, the habits that stayed behind when she left. He won't do anything in fours. Won't remove a cricket from the house. The summer is thick with crickets and Kate can catch them in her hands now. Not even flinching at their dry bodies or the frantic little scratches on her palms as she carries them out to the yard.

He tells Kate it took a long time to end. It ended properly on the night that Sonja reached over from the passenger seat and grabbed the wheel so hard they nearly slammed into a Mercedes in the next lane. Though sometimes Kate's not sure if the story about grabbing the steering wheel is something he has told her, or something she was afraid to tell him. Either way, she feels like a story he has already heard. Kate remembers what it felt like to grab the wheel, to truly want the car to crash. She remembers what it felt like to throw herself against walls.

When Sonja left she took the cat and moved to a small apartment overlooking the park. Kate once lived alone with a cat in a small apartment overlooking a park. She once took the same medication as Sonja. When she runs out of razors she uses one of the razors Sonja left behind. She has tried on the winter coat and stood in front of the hallway mirror, her hands balled into fists in the pockets. The sleeves of the coat don't reach her wrists. She knows this isn't supposed to mean anything.

On the afternoons that Kate runs she does laps around the park, looking up at the windows of the surrounding apartment buildings. All the windows reflect the glare of the setting sun, so she can't see through them, but she feels that Sonja is behind one of them. Sitting very still with her knees drawn up to her chin and the cat beside her. Saying, Look. Just because you once lived alone with a cat in a small apartment over-looking a park. Just because you know what my blood looks like. Doesn't mean you know me.

Suitable for a lampshade

I got the call when I was too far away to do anything about it. There was a pile of marking to get through that I knew I wouldn't get through, but that had been the case even before the call.

I'd rented a holiday house from a friend of a friend. And they'd probably bought it and all its contents from the children of an elderly deceased lady, or of one who had recently been moved to an aged care facility, because the bookcases were still crammed with Reader's Digest omnibuses and craft books; *Advanced Macramé*, *Crocheted Endings*. Also the kitchen cupboards were stacked with earthenware plates and mismatched glassware and crockery, and these anodised aluminium cups that reminded me of the photographic version of my childhood, which is really nothing like the childhood I can actually remember.

The rent was only one hundred and twenty-five a week because I was a friend of a friend and because it was the middle of June. The wind came right off the Pacific to whine under the door sills and through the gaps between the old weatherboards, and to rattle the windows in their poorly made frames.

I'd gone there to dry out, from you as much as anything else. Okay, from you and only you, because I was still drinking and I had no intention of drying that out. Straight vodka or watered whisky out of the little blue anodised cups, which I considered taking with me when I left. It was inherited bric-a-brac, after all, and this friend of a friend hadn't had time to develop any real emotional attachment to any of it. So the cups, and to a lesser extent the books on crochet and macramé, and some sixties plastic swizzle sticks I'd found in the third kitchen drawer – I was already thinking of those things as mine.

I was trying not to think about you. I had all this work to do and I'd bought a pair of glasses with small lenses and thick frames so that only a limited amount of the world was in focus at any one time. I thought they might minimise peripheral distraction, help me keep my attention on what was in front of me. You probably know it didn't work out that way. But the glasses made me look like someone who drank Laphroaig instead of Jameson and worked from a typewriter instead of a laptop, and I liked that.

There was no good place to buy coffee near to the house, so there was no good reason to leave it. I made drink ice in the freezer of the ancient Kelvinator and read most of a book on anaesthesia that was written in the forties, and if those things didn't keep me happy they at least kept me a reasonable and safe distance from unhappy. I'd say anaesthetised, but that would be too obvious and not entirely true. I played chess and Scrabble against myself, and the essays on Jeffers and Riding stayed unread and unmarked on the kitchen table.

In the weeks I was there the sky never grew any lighter than the colour of bruised mushrooms, and if I drove to the ocean it was grey and hungry in the James Reeves sort of way. Maybe every second or third day I drove to the ocean and just sat in the driver's seat, watching the container ships crawling after each other so I could tell where the horizon was, though most days the sea was the same colour as the sky and if not for the ships you wouldn't have known any difference between the two.

Some afternoons there was a girl on the sand with her dog, a black wolfish mongrel she'd throw pieces of driftwood for. He churned the wet grey sand up under his paws, chasing after whatever she threw.

Yeah, I thought. I know how that is. I know exactly how.

And down on the beach the wind pulled at them, made their hair and her loose clothing ripple. Like the two of them were only shapes cut from cloth.

Cloth girl with her cloth dog. My fingers would always creep to the door handle but wouldn't push it down.

Yes, it was because she looked like you. There are worse reasons for wanting to talk to someone. Because they look like they have money, or they're beautiful or they look like somebody famous – those are worse reasons.

Anyway, it was because she reminded me of you that I finally got out of the car and went down to the beach to ask her about her dog, or whether she lived nearby or something similar. Maybe I asked if she knew a good place to get coffee. I don't remember what I asked because, whatever it was, she didn't answer it. She just pushed her hair off her face and asked if I was the one driving that blue Skyline. All her clothes were shapeless and only the wind whipping the fabric up close to her skin brought any kind of definition.

When I nodded she said, Yeah, I thought so, and threw a stick for the dog. Nobody just watches the ocean. Not in this weather.

I'm just watching the ocean, I said. The dog came back with the stick. Why, what are you doing in this weather?

I'm just walking my dog, she said. He doesn't give a damn about the weather. Sweet stupid thing, and she threw the stick again. Then she smiled and looked at me from behind her wind-whipped hair. Maybe, she said. Maybe you're just watching the ocean.

And I was still trying not to think about you, or the holiday house I'd once rented with you; its own mismatched glassware, or how we'd made love against kitchen benches and spat gin into each other's mouths. Carrying everything back out to the car on the morning we left, your tired grin above a box of groceries we hadn't managed to get through, or the carton of bottles that we had.

But it was no good and I remembered everything. The arguments, the ugly carpet. The way the sound of the hot water system found its way into our dreams and we dreamed of the same things for six nights. How the firewood had been cut from old railway sleepers, and the bolts glowed red hot among the embers. Sleeping in the car at the side of the highway on the way home. The trucks shuddering by and your breath clouding the window, the early light cold, almost blue, and oh god – if I could have kept things just like that. If I could have stopped time at the side of the Hume with you sleeping and your hair across your face and me just watching you sleeping, the trucks shuddering past. Well, you know I would have.

I think maybe the girl knew this. Maybe even knew that she reminded me of you, but she was good about it. Or she didn't have to be good about it, because she didn't care either way. Her dog lay on the wooden decking outside with his legs stretched out ahead of him, and when I said that he could come in she said, No, he can't, and he stayed out there, looking woeful. It seems strange to me now that I never learned the dog's name. It could have been Samson or Solomon, something biblical. The girl shook the rain out of her coat and left it by the door.

Then when the call came through, she was asleep on her stomach, her long legs still slightly parted and the damp sheet pulled up across the backs of her knees. I stumbled naked to the front room with the phone, not wanting to wake her, tripping over a powerboard, a lone shoe. When I answered my voice sounded thin and hostile. I stood looking out the window. The sky had grown dark and the dog had fallen asleep out on the decking. There was the pile of paperwork that had never left its manila folder, and your mother on the line asking why I hadn't answered the home phone or the work phone, why I hadn't returned any of her damn messages.

Three days, she said, and as she kept talking all I could think about was how I should have gotten out of the car that morning. I should have walked along the highway and thumbed a ride back to Melbourne with one of the truck drivers. Then you would still be asleep in the passenger seat. The light would still be almost blue, your hair just-so across your face, and this little cluttered house with its storm and its sleeping dog and its anodised aluminium cups would be a dream you were having. I would be standing naked at the window of the dream, watching the sky grow dark. There would be a box of groceries on your back seat, and you would be okay. You would be safe.

Your mother said *sudden*. She said *collapse*, she said *supermarket fucking car park*, and I don't remember how I answered any of that. I don't remember what I said before hanging up. Just that after I'd hung up, I pulled a book down from the shelf and turned to Chapter Three: Suitable for a lampshade, or a handkerchief. And how I just stood there with the book open at page sixty-two, waiting for those words to mean something.

Treacherous

Her clavicles. Once they jutted out so far you couldn't look at them without imagining treacherous mountain passes covered in snow, tiny armies marching down either side to a war in her suprasternal notch. Then she fleshed out a bit, and the war was over (more or less).

View

His eyes were not good. This didn't matter to him anymore. His eyes had once worked fine, and it had mattered when the deterioration began, but he had grown used to it since then. He could still see a little – colours and shapes without definition or depth. As if he were standing too close to an impressionist painting. When he stood looking out of the window of his front room, the mountains folded into each other like soft grey flannel, with no hint of abrasion or human interference. But he had lived in the same house for thirty years, and what his eyes could not see of the mountains his memory substituted, and he knew them to be scarred with walking tracks, quarried in places and blackened in others, weary with people. On the northwestern face there had once been a landslide. One snaggled ghost gum jutted slantways out of the bare rock, and he still thought it there, still wondered which way the roots grew and if bad weather would ever bring it down.

This was the view he had bought, along with the house, the property. The view remained unchanged throughout the birth, growth and eventual departure of his daughter, and throughout the illness and inevitable death of his wife. The house felt the emptiness of the past few years, and compensated for it by falling in on itself, but the view was still his. Even blindness would not take it from him.

Other senses had sharpened as his sight had failed. He knew by sound and smell how high the gas range was, could hear his daughter's car engine long before it reached the driveway. Alison came by three or four times a week with groceries, and to cook and freeze his meals. When his sight first began to weaken, and grew so weak that he could no longer read, she read aloud to him. Mostly newspaper articles or short stories by William Faulkner and Patrick White.

Too old now, he had said, to start learning Braille.

But she read too softly, and he complained that she did not own the words when she read them. Now she brought him audio books on cassette from the public library, some read by their authors and others by voice actors. Sometimes the stories were no good, or the voice of the reader did not fit that of the character. He would swear and shuffle over to the player to stop the tape before the end of the first chapter. But when the books were good, or when they were not very good but were read well, he would lean back in his chair with his eyelids closed, and he would see very clearly their Mississippi dust and Chickasaw chiefs, their woven nets and hardened women. He would forget his failed vision. Then when the side had ended and the voice stopped, he would open his eyes and see the mountains soft and grey as heaped ash and he would know that the softness was only an illusion, just a trick of his eyes. In his mind he would see the lone ghost gum, growing from the sheer wall of rock but resolute and still bearing leaves, and he would wonder which way the roots grew.

When his daughter was there he would ask her, Tell me about the view.

The mountains?

Yes. Tell me about the mountains. Tell me if anything's changed.

They look how they always have.

And that ghost gum?

It's still there. Nothing's changed.

Which way do you s'pose the roots grow?

Towards water, Dad.

Up or down? Or further in?

I couldn't tell you.

But it's still there?

I told you.

He would feel a strange relief trickle through him, slow-burning like peated whisky, and he could see then the scars of the walking tracks and remember walking them with Alison's mother through the blackened and quarried places when his eyes were still good and the summer crackled around them. He remembered Alison's mother with sun showing through her fine hair and through her dress, and the dust that rose as she walked and stuck with the sheen of sweat on her bare calves. He would not allow himself to remember any more than that. Before he remembered any more than that he would scrape through the basket of cassette tapes or turn on the radio and listen to the news, or the weather, even the talkback he hated, until the memory was blurred with the same softness as the mountains and his own hands were made strange – familiar in shape and colour, but annulled of detail, of scars and history.

His eyes became worse. Alison started coming five or six times a week although he told her not to. There were things that had lost possession of him – time in particular, and appearance to some extent – and when Alison came she brought these things with her. But she also brought the audio books, so he let her fuss with the washing and the meals and on and on about his smoking and his appetite. Alison's mother had never fussed so much. She hadn't minded him smoking. But he had his sight then. Perhaps if she'd have lived long enough to see him going blind, things might have been different. He let Alison go on fussing.

★

It was during a spring of heavy rainfall and power failures. Alison had called on him during a blackout, and after persuading her to go home for the evening he had lit the candles out of habit and used the batteries from the smoke alarm to power the radio. The batteries died and he sat awake all night in the quiet dark, the sound of the storm and of the house groaning around him every so often, as if in troubled sleep. As if it might stir from that sleep, murmur something to itself and roll over, him inside it.

When the tree came down he heard it. Heard it in such precise detail that, although his own hands were now strange to him and he could not read the face of the watch he still wore, he saw the startled birds erupting from the tilting canopy as one screeching white flurry against the grey pre-dawn sky. He saw the earth wrenched from the side of the mountain, the clumps of clay and rock held in the tangled mass of the root system, and the small insects that moved through the exposed clay.

Then when the morning came he saw the blur of the soft grey mountains. And he knew that their softness was not real, but could no longer remember them otherwise.

Swan dive

All those mornings, our bodies slicked with a sugary sweat. Pure alcohol. You could've tasted the night before just by licking our wrists. Stella arcing back so the girls could do body shots from between her perfect breasts. The men drinking and watching, *You're a flexible little thing, aren't you sweetheart?*

We were inexhaustible in those final few months, throwing ourselves around every chance we got. Our heads might've rolled off and we wouldn't have noticed. Mine probably did. Amanda and Stella started dancing at the Foxhouse two or three nights a week because the money was good and our rent was insane. Then it was three or four nights. They'd show up at the studio in the morning still smelling of tipping dollars. It's okay if you're smart about it, they said, stretching at the barre. If you don't hate it enough to start looking for ways to forget about it.

You should think on it, said Stella, who was spending half the week as Lola.

That accent. They'd eat it up. Amanda was Ruby from Thursday to Saturday.

A swan dive, I guess you could call it.

Sometimes I want to tell you about this, but I won't. How the hours slammed up against each other. I'd never seen so many sunrises. We'd peel away our damp costumes and step straight into three-dollar g-strings that were only good for a few nights, until the lace was discoloured with sweat. The other girls at the club told us we should stick to darker colours; black, navy, even red. Then we wouldn't be going through so many pairs. But we knew what we were doing. Pale blue. Sugar pink. White, white, white. Let them think we were angelic. We knew how to be angelic.

Hotels

They live in hotels for a while, after he does that to her face. Not real bad, but bad enough for them to leave the same night. Frantically packing the car as though hoping to outrun some unknowable natural disaster. There's sand in the bed, Baby, he's saying. Back at the house, a million years ago in the suburbs. And she won't tell him why. She's letting him believe things. There's sand in the bed, and they are a long way from the ocean.

He tucks a blanket around her shoulders and they drive three hours, past the bedroom communities in the west, his hand on her thigh and the radio on. When he speaks it's as though he were speaking to a child he hopes to befriend, and she answers as a child might, imagining her child-self running down the dark stretch of highway alongside the passenger window of their white Hyundai. Pushing her breath out ahead of her, never tiring. Never turning her head to meet the eyes of the passenger, who is unravelling a loose thread from her skirt and saying, No, I don't suppose work would miss me for a little while.

At the first hotel she waits in the car while he speaks with the concierge. On the radio the Mills Brothers are singing about Sadie Green. Twee twee twee twah twah, and she falls asleep briefly, jerking awake when he comes back for her and the bags. She follows him through the hotel foyer to the lift, her hair pulled down over one side of her face.

They drink steadily in the first few days. Glasses stationed around the room with dried half-moons of lime in the bottom. So hot out that the tint is blistering off the windows of cars in the street. But that is out in the great, dusty world that they are not a part of for the moment. The insides of the hotels are cool and stark, and there is nothing to remind them of themselves. Their luggage lost in the mirrored halls of wardrobes. The bed a vast white plane where nothing terrible has ever happened, where they lie naked on the bright sheets and he tries to lift the bruises from her face with remedies he has heard or read about. Butter, honey, kaffir lime. And although she knows none of it will work, she smiles and lets him. The bruise remains and blackens, but they wake each morning to clean light with only the slightest recollection of the dreams they have climbed out of.

When he goes out for fresh limes, for fresh bottles of gin and soda water, she watches his back as he moves across the car park. Already sweating, looking back at the hotel every now and then, although it's obvious he can't tell which window she's standing behind, which room is theirs.

A playground, she thinks, or a building site – she knows she could have said anything about the sand. That he wanted to believe her. Disasters with egg timers, he would have believed even that. But she'd panicked and said nothing, and he'd taken hold of her shoulders and shook her, hard, so that her head nodded loosely on her neck as he shouted Why? Why? Why?

Now they are here, and his brother is looking after their dog.

After several days there is hair in the sink, stains on the sheets. Unwashed clothes piling up on the floor. This grittiness an emissary from their life before the hotels, threatening the equilibrium he has charged to the joint account. At these first traces of disarray they move on, him packing their belongings with the same urgency as when leaving the house, only to arrive at another version of the first hotel. Only to fall onto another bed where no smell or stain of either of them is held in the memory of its sheets. These rooms so sterile that nothing could fester. Though nothing could possibly grow, she thinks. She is inside a parenthesis, where nothing matters yet, no decisions need to be made. But she is always thirsty in these places, each night waking sticky-mouthed and sliding from beneath his outflung arm. Each night drinking from her cupped hands and watching her reflection in the bathroom mirror, sometimes dabbing at her cheekbone with wet fingertips. Under the halogen lights the bruise looks like bad theatrical make-up; two weeks now and it hasn't rubbed away, and she's lost count of the places they've stayed in. This could be the fourth or the fifth. The hotels fit neatly inside each other like matryoshka dolls. Half-sized, quarter-sized. The first hotel turned from a single piece of wood, solid as a nut and sealed up tight.

She saw a quarter-sized hotel once; public art at the side of a freeway somewhere south of here. She had wanted to pull over, to crawl in there on her hands and knees and lay her head on one of the scaled-down beds. To sleep for a long time, dreamless and alone, in a place where no one would find her.

If she could get back there. Take the keys from his jacket while he sleeps, and head south. Inside the quarter-sized hotel it would be empty, just bracing and wires for the neon lights, but it wouldn't matter. She could drive all night and be there by late morning. She would begin to remember. It would be as simple as that.

Heart of gold

Lana drove all four of us out to the desert just so she could toss her shoes up into a tree. It took her three goes – *hah. hah. hah!* – and by the third try she was crying hard.

Why'd you do that, said Mira. Those shoes are too good for that tree.

We looked up into the branches slung with old running shoes and scuffed-up boots, and down where some of them lay in the dust beneath the tree, their laces frayed where they'd snapped. Mira was right; Lana's shoes didn't belong there. But she just ran her skinny wrist under her nose and said, Let's go back now, okay? She walked shoeless back to the car and got in on the driver's side. On the trip back we kept schtum, avoiding her sooty eyes in the rearview mirror. We watched her bare feet working the accelerator and clutch. When we stopped for fuel we watched her stand barefoot on the grease-stained concrete while she filled the tank, then we watched her dance barefoot down the service station aisles. Heart of Gold was playing over the loudspeakers as she swung slow and sad past the confectionary, past the ice-cream freezer. We watched the soles of her feet get blacker and blacker, picking up grime from the tiled floor. We tried our best to make sense of it.

Raising the wreck

They're raising the wreck. After so many years of it brooding innocuously beneath the surface, some idiot's jet ski collided with it at low tide last September. Thao would be devastated. All morning people have been gathering on the beach to watch. Some have come prepared with picnics, cameras, binoculars, beer. Others are empty-handed passersby, joggers and intended swimmers who were turned back from the water. A few small-time journos are mooching through the crowd, interviewing locals about their memories of scrabbling onto the stern when it was still jutting out above the water. Of slipping and lacerating their arm or their foot on the mussel shells. Rolling back a sleeve, Here, here's the scar.

David sits beside me on the sand, lounging back against the dinged-up esky that is holding cold chicken sandwiches and a few bottles of pale ale. His white linen shirt is unbuttoned and flapping loose, but who's looking. He leafs through the first few scenes of the play, deciphering my furious little squiggles.

Would you say, he asks, that this . . . infatuation? Okay, this *interest* that he had, would you say it came from him feeling like something of an outsider?

Divers are surfacing beside the salvage vessel, then disappearing again, trailing cables down to the seabed to snake around the ruined hull.

I'm sure he'd be thrilled for us to think so. Do you think those beers are cold yet?

When they brought him in from casting. Holy cats. They'd brought in a lot of guys who looked like Thao, but they didn't speak or move like Thao. This kid even smelled like Thao. When I shook his hand there was a whiff of smoke and dry grass. *You smell like an arsonist*, I told Thao once. And he'd given me that grin, parenthesised by the lines around his mouth. Like a hammock strung between two young birches who were leaning under its weight. The same as this kid was giving me, still holding onto my hand.

I've read your book, he said. Three times now. Feels almost like I know you.

If you could spend some time with him, Georgia had asked before introducing me to David. Tell him how things were for the two of you. Be honest with him.

And without knowing what a unique form of torture it would be, I said yes.

Good, Georgia said. So much gets lost in translation,
don't you think? Just reading the book, I mean.

What about the person playing me, do I sit down
with them too?

We haven't found a 'you' yet, Alex. But yes, that
would be very helpful.

Georgia never passes on an opportunity to remind me
how lucky I am to be involved in the production, that
writers are typically considered nuisances at this stage
of development and are only to be consulted as to the
filling of plot holes and the ironing out of other minor
dilemmas. Chandler's Law, Chekhov's Gun and what
have you. I never pass on an opportunity to remind
Georgia that she is twenty-fucking-six, and greener
than her Green Room Award. Still has that Melbourne
smugness wavering about her like heat haze. In any
case, there are no men bursting into rooms with loaded
revolvers and double entendres in my book. No Lauren
Bacall trying to hold up her unsteady head. Just Thao
and my life with him, at least a version of it. Of our life
together, until the night he swam out, drunk, to the
wreck.

It wasn't so long ago that the wreckage could be seen
at low tide, just the tip of it sticking out of the water, a
long way from shore. But it had collapsed in on itself in

the early thousands, collapsed or shifted position, rolling over like a dog wanting to have its belly scratched, and it was no longer visible from the beach. The idea of swimming out to it always terrified me. I justified this terror with common sense; riptides, inevitable fatigue. I was – I am – no great swimmer. But it was never the fear of drowning that stopped me, rather the thought of the wreck itself, the rusting barnacled hull, all the unknowable things it was harbouring. Dark thoughts of a shape that I couldn't fit words to.

But I would watch Thao, from the safety of our sandy chequered rug, and I would watch the other beachgoers and the tourists watching him, the children who paddled behind him like dolphins in the wake of a ship before they grew tired or fearful or their parents called them back in. Thao had been swimming out to it since he was a child, and could always find it, no matter the conditions. In the water he was a beautiful machine, hardly turning his head from the water to breathe.

He'd come back when he was ready, to stand over the rug, chest heaving, his hammock-shaped smile. I always wanted to pull him down onto me, taste the salt on him. But he was so discreet in public. He'd fall onto the rug, bat my hands away.

Tell me something, Thao.

Six deaths a year are caused by rabbits.

That's fascinating. Please, go on.

Thao's parents, who did not speak to me when Thao was alive, continued to not speak to me after his death. I don't know if they have ever read the book, whether they avoided bookstore window displays for the few weeks that it occupied space there. They had wanted many things for Thao, and I was not one of them.

A man, his mother had said. A man is one thing. But an old man? Your father and I do not deserve this.

I see his father's picture in the paper sometimes. I look for the signs of loss in his face. A volcanologist, he is consulted mostly during times of disaster. Yet he has not aged as I have aged, these past eight years.

After I found out Thao was dead I packed all of his things into a box, thinking somebody was going to come and collect them, and when no one did I unpacked them again. I returned his shirts to the wardrobe, his jeans and socks and underwear to the drawers I had hesitantly cleared for him two years earlier.

When David wants to know something, he doesn't hesitate. He has read the book, and it's all in there, I remind myself. It's all for show, doesn't belong to anybody anymore. David asks how Thao would stand if he were waiting for something. Whether he was a loud talker or a soft talker. Whether he ate with his hands. The shape his mouth made when he came. Most things I don't have an answer for. Most things I have to make up.

I invite him home to show him Thao's clothes and his trashy thrillers that had wriggled their way into my bookshelves. I show him the grey earth in the back garden, from which Thao had coaxed basil, parsley, the feathery gills of dill, coriander that he replanted every fortnight in summer, as it went to seed so quickly. On the kitchen table I smooth out brittle newspaper clippings of the World War II naval mine Thao had found almost thirty years ago, massive and urcheonlike amongst the coral. He had known that it was very old – *tired*, he said, from drifting around the Pacific for so many years, broken free from the chain which had once anchored it to the sea floor. *Itinerant*, was another word that he used, which always brought to my mind the addition of a battered leather suitcase and a waterlogged bowler hat, though I never joked about this with Thao. He'd swum out to meet it every day for a week before finally telling his father, a fervent alerter of proper authorities. The mine was carefully extracted from the reef, and detonated offshore a week later. Thao, who had never been allowed pets, recalled this incident in the manner that others recall euthanised animals sent to fictitious farms.

Must you befriend all the salty old ruins? I asked him.

Georgia is ambivalent when it comes to the subject of the mine.

I mean, how do you stage that? How do you stage it

without ruining it? She shakes her head. I don't want it to look like a high school production.

I can see him clearly, skinny arms around his bony knees, conversing silently with the mine beneath the surface of the water.

It's already been ruined, George. I ruined it by writing it. Thao ruined it by telling me. It might as well be ruined some more.

Alex. Georgia looks into my face. You are a sad, sad man. Anyway, I don't think it's in the budget. Maybe we'll just have Thao talk about it.

You mean David.

I mean Thao, who is being played by David. Are you getting precious?

Right. No, I'm not precious.

There are things I want to ask David. There are moments when I think he will be able to answer. I want to ask him what Thao saw, whether it was bright enough for him to see anything at all, there in the oil-black water. Whether it calmed him, laying his hands against the great hull of the dead ship. Feeling something like a heartbeat as the tide pulsed inside it. I know he might not have made it out that far. I like to think that he did, though I'm not sure why it matters, either way. He washed up on some doctor's private beach. Or what some doctor thought of as her private beach. I had to read about it.

Onstage, Alex is demolishing the fourth wall. I've decided that I don't much like Alex. Everything he says sounds pantomimic. It's all I can do to not shout out, He's behind you, you fool!

It was not a compulsion, he tells the audience, which just now consists of Georgia and myself. Not a need that I had for sexual conquest or variety. Just a fundamental interest in other people's lives, and how they lived them. The stories they told themselves through the photographs and possessions they chose to display. I wanted the kind of insight that came with nights spent awake in strangers' houses . . .

Georgia hollers down at the stage every now and then, I want to see more regret there. Again please, and can we have a longer pause this time?

I sit beside her with a printout of the script, making a shuddery little mark at every point that I fail to conceal a bodily cringe.

Our final argument is being staged in a lounge room. For reasons pertaining to aesthetics, the lounge room looks nothing like my lounge room, despite the images I sent through. Not really cluttery enough for a writer, was the logic.

For reasons pertaining to dramatic structure, we are having a final argument.

In truth, there was no final argument. I did not come home, and then Thao did not come home. When I slept my dreams were of massive ships being launched from slipways, listing dangerously before righting themselves like toys. I took it as a good omen. Three days later, after a few dozen unanswered phone calls and text messages, the reply crashed into the gardenias along with the Saturday supplements.

Thao sways out from the shadows. You, he says, are a fucking scavenger. Chewing pieces out of other people's lives. You know what good writers do? They make shit up. They use their imagination.

At the word imagination, Thao jams his index finger against my temple. Holds it there like a pistol while I say, No. All writers are scavengers. The good and the bad.

Perhaps it would have been better like this.

Georgia turns to me in the dark. Is there anything you'd like to add, Alex?

Nothing, I tell her. Thank you.

David takes two beers from the esky, uncaps the first with the second and hands it to me, then paws around in the ice for the bottle opener. He rakes his hair back with wet fingers, shades his eyes from the glare coming off the water.

Out there, the stern is once again visible. Then the keel, and the hull, water gushing from the damage. They haul it up until it hangs in the air, glistening and terrible. I get a good look at it then; draped with weed, armoured in limpet. *The thing itself and not the myth.*

Then a cable breaks, and the whole twisted mess of it crashes back into the water.

Repairs

She took the 'S' arm off her typewriter so that she wouldn't be able to spell his name. It would help, she thought. If only in a small, stupid way. But she couldn't spell her own name, without the 'S', and this was problematic. Her name, and a lot of other names, a lot of other words.

Bezt. Regardz. Cheerz. Xincerely. Thanx.

The typewriter repairman came to work each day in a suit which had once fit him well. He sat amongst the boxes of new ribbons and the cans of compressed air, the refurbished Underwoods and Olivettis, and he waited. He knew a lot of things that didn't matter anymore, such as how to repair a broken carriage pull, how to realign typebars and how to reattach those that had been torn off in fits of anger or fits of despair. When she came in with her S-less Corona, he pushed his glasses further up the bridge of his nose.

Love, then? he asked, as she lowered the old machine onto his workbench.

Probably, she said. Probably love. Sorry to make you do this again.

House

When I write of a house now, it is only ever the one house: its smell of smoke and old wood, foxed books, dried bluegum torn lazily from the overgrown yard. Perhaps you haven't realised this yet. Because in one story, I've sat you at the monstrous kitchen table, its surface a forest of knives, their tips driven into the southern mahogany. The empty knife block hidden amongst them like the woodcutter's empty cottage. And in another story, we are crouched behind the ruined shed, amongst the blood and the feathers, and from here the kitchen cannot be seen. Stand in the birdless aviary (you know where we are now, don't you?) and you won't see me lying on the slate floor, won't feel my hands either side of your face. You won't hear me saying there isn't a single thing I feel sorry about. It's only ever the one house, but it's shifting, unmappable, and I can never get far enough away to see the whole of it.

Into the arms of the parade

I went into her apartment and there was nothing on the walls. Just one bright room with ruined floorboards, and no furniture in the room except an easel, a bookshelf stacked with ragged paperbacks and a four-panel folding screen with a mattress behind it. The screen was exquisite and didn't belong in the room; its wooden panels slid into the framework and were carved to look like the boughs of a willow tree. The mattress didn't make it any easier to imagine someone living in that space. Waking up there, under the pile of blankets. Eating while standing, like a horse, looking out of the one narrow window. She was twice my age, at least – too old to live like that. I laced my fingers through the leaves of the wooden screen while she set up the easel and scraped at a stick of charcoal.

She said to sit anywhere, but there was nowhere to sit. I undressed and leaned against the window sill, my back turned on the view of inner suburban rooftops and the bare branches of the plane trees. On a neighbouring roof a small forest had taken root in the build-up of dead leaves and bird shit. The owners of the house probably didn't even know it was up there, but sparrows were darting in and out and making their homes amongst the spindly growth. Yes, beautiful things still happened by accident. It could happen just like that. I had my head in that incidental forest, small birds scratching at the sides of my thoughts, but my eyes were fixed on the second row of the bookshelf, where a postcard showing a Mexican parade was propped against the cracked spines of Pessoa and le Carré. I thought that if I could only flip it over and read what was written on the back, I might be able to know something about her. Perhaps a greater knowing than she could have of me, seeing only my pale breasts and the burn scar on my thigh, the silver tendrils creeping out across my stomach, marking where the skin had stretched, uselessly.

It's not how you'd think, never sexual. It's more like being topography, or furniture, or both – like being a landscape carved into a folding screen. I've learned to measure time through pain and paraesthesia, in how a raised arm will fall asleep right up to the shoulder in less than ten minutes, depending on blood pressure. For me it's six minutes.

The fingers of my left hand were already tingling and I was looking at the Mexican postcard, thinking about something stupid I'd said to somebody the night before. I turned the conversation over and over behind the blank expression I was holding, sure that she could see the whole exchange playing out behind my eyes. When I was still for long periods of time it always happened this way. Like televised violence I couldn't turn my head from. Old failures and humiliations broke loose from their moorings and bobbed to the surface, as if up from dark water. If I stood up and moved around I could shake them for a while, but they'd be waiting when I settled back into position, as though it were not a chair or a chaise longue or a window sill I was returning to, but a great hall where all of my mistakes lined the walls, waiting for their turn to grab my wrist. I looked at the dancing women of the Mexican postcard, their plump arms extending from the ruffled sleeves of Adelita dresses. Reaching skyward, as if to catch something considered unanimously precious.

After twenty minutes I stretched and rolled my ankles, listening to the bones crack. I opened and closed my left hand, waiting for the blood to come back to it. Then I walked around behind her canvas to see whether I looked anything like myself. In twenty minutes, she'd only sketched as far as my left clavicle, part of my shoulder and a procession of tiny boats wrecked beneath my suprasternal notch. The boats were all empty, skeletal. Their sterns and skegs rotted, and the oars torn away. I felt uneasy then, as though she'd slipped a palette knife under my collarbone and prised it up like it was an old floorboard to see what was underneath.

Do you still need me to stand here if you're only drawing boats? I asked.

She didn't answer, and I stood beside her a moment longer before returning to my place by the window, setting the timer for another twenty minutes and biting the inside of my cheek to keep myself there, in her stark apartment, or in the fleshy arms of Central Mexico. Anywhere but that crowded hall. I thought of Eva Frederick, her hands folded forever across her soft belly in museum storage rooms, and no one knowing a single thing about her that wasn't right there, in either of the two portraits Kahlo had made out of her.

My name's not even Elena, I said without turning my head. That's not even Elena's shoulder you're drawing.

The artist finally looked out from behind her easel. Whose is it then?

It's somebody else's. That's my point. You don't even know whose shoulder you're drawing, so why do you need me here to continue on with your boats?

What difference does it make? She asked this gently, reassuring. What difference could it possibly make?

I leaned back imperceptibly, so that my shoulder blades touched the cool glass of the window. I was still looking at the postcard, and although I couldn't read what was written on the back of it I felt I could see into all the corners of her life. Past the battered paperbacks and the beautiful folding screen. Through the willow boughs to the mattress under its heaped blankets, straight through to the tangled sadness of sleep. Behind me the windowpane had warmed with the heat of my body, until it seemed as though the glass might melt and I could at last fall back, numb, into the arms of the parade.

Souvenirs

Unspookable

When you come back you won't know me. I swear to god I don't even stand the way I used to. Nothing to send a ripple out across my flesh like I was a startled horse about to bolt, not anymore. You only got so much nerves, my father said once, and when they're worn through they're worn through. And I know what he meant – that you're supposed to go to pieces then, when all your nerve is gone, but it didn't happen that way for me. My nerves got worn through and then I didn't have to worry about them again. The wind kicks dust in my face and I don't even blink, you understand. I'm unflinching now. Unspookable.

I kept souvenirs from the time before, things to know my old self by in case it ever came limping back. Pieces of the kids' clothes. Blueprints of the house and the registration papers for the car, as though the past were a place I could return to if I was holding the right documents. The wedding ring they had to cut away in the emergency ward.

My hands got burned up pretty bad. My hands and my arms. It was too late anyway and it didn't prove a thing but it felt right at the time. I couldn't just not do anything. And I know people are looking at me now, different from how they once did, cause I look like someone who's got a story. But it's not a story anyone would want to know. Not like I know it, word for word and breath for breath. The exact weight and shape of it so that even my hands remember. My hands have a memory all of their own and they keep raising up as though to stop the things they couldn't stop.

But you can hold them if you want to. They don't hurt anymore.

A kind of ritual

She'd already started going to pieces the year the Southern Star melted, its twelve hundred tonnes of steel buckling in the January heatwave. The attraction was dismantled and hauled off somewhere, leaving only the support towers and lateral bracing.

It was as though the wheel had simply rolled away one night, slipping quietly past the ice-skating rink and the direct factory outlets. Into the Yarra River, churning up the mud under the West Gate Bridge and travelling on out into Port Phillip Bay, before finally settling on its side with its tail in its mouth; an exhausted, ouroboric beast.

He remembers thinking about it afterwards, and the peace it had brought him then. The idea of something so large disappearing so quickly, that the world was bigger than his own mistakes. That the world would forget them. But the remnants of the structure looming over the docklands are a hulking monument to failures inseparable from his own. A reminder of the warning signs he missed and the things he can't bring back.

Each time he drives across the Bolte Bridge he feels something like a fist closing inside his chest. Twice a day, five days of the week. He will sometimes lift his hand from the steering wheel as he passes. Salute the life he once had, repeat the names of his children like a broken mantra. It's become a kind of ritual. Moving forward without leaving.

Yes they remember

Yes they remember the dogs the smell of their paws and their sighs that meant nothing the sound of them clattering through the house and round the yard all the things they helped to bury things no one will ever find now the bird bones the broken cups their grandfather's watch with its tick slowed to the sound of a heart Yes they remember the yard lying face-down on it its earth and its secrets the dryness of their final summer smell of sunscreen rotting magnolia insecticide the dead-grass smell of circuses of animal pavilions Yes they remember the summer the scratch of split vinyl back seat on salt dry cheeks and the weight of the coats they slept under sand pouring from the pockets on the way back from the ocean Yes they remember the ocean being thrown from strong shoulders and scrambling up to be thrown again the world tilting and the water meeting them a dozen different ways they have these pictures now of days stuck like they were cut from magazines and cannot tell whose was whose the lion in the glass box rope swing by a yellow river cicada shells clinging to rough tree bark and their names etched into the damp wood of the jetty but whose was whose? whose lip split on the handlebars whose arm torn by the loose nail Yes they remember the taste of blood the spit the stitches their mother fainting but all of this is fainting all of it fragile now like the bird they found one morning with its heart slowed to a dull knock to the tick of an earthbound clock and they can cup it all in their hands all of it (the bird the ocean the summer the dogs) and breathe their warm breath on it try to keep it alive a while longer but they can't take it with them they can't take any of it with them and out in the yard there are the things that they buried all the things they would one day come back for.

Scar from a trick with a knife

We were embarrassed by your kindness. You insisted we take the bed, saying the floor would do you fine, and in the spare room of your small apartment you lay on an inflatable camping mattress, surrounded by our equipment and luggage. Maybe you liked that – the forest of tripods; soft mountains of clothing and towels spilling from our suitcases; forty-two inch reflector rising like a full moon behind it all. Maybe it felt like being part of something important. Or maybe we were flattering ourselves, thinking that. We had money from a town you'd never been to, for a project we had difficulty explaining.

So you are here to make photographs of hands?

Yes.

Hands only?

Mostly hands, yes.

And this is for helping people in your country to understand . . . ?

About collective residual guilt.

Collective. Residual. Guilt. Old people's hands or younger people's hands?

Anyone's hands. It doesn't matter.

My hands also?

Sure, you have great hands.

And they would help people to understand?

Definitely.

But I do not feel guilty.

But of course we didn't believe you, because there was still the inexplicable kindness. You weren't even religious. We needed to find reasons for it. Like you'd done something horrendous earlier in your life that you were working to make amends for. We would have been satisfied with that.

It was something we noticed immediately, shaking hands with you on the platform of Schönleinstraße. Just as if it were a speech impediment or disproportionate features. But you looked and sounded normal; fine blonde hair thinning at your temples, pale skin, bad posture from the desk job you hated to talk about. Brief smile, like headlights from a slow-moving car sweeping over a lounge-room wall at night time. And the same grey-blue eyes as the cousin who had given us your email address. It wasn't a physical thing, but it was just as obvious. A person could have made it out from across the street, or by glimpsing your face in the window of a passing train. We called it loneliness because we couldn't think of a better word for it at the time, though retrospectively we called it *apartness* – something that had possibly developed out of loneliness, but more likely the other way around – and we didn't notice we'd both noticed this until some time later, talking quietly together in your bed. Our heads on your pillows, discussing it; your apartness. How you must have hoped to compensate for it with your kindness, and how the kindness only drew attention to it. Yes, it felt wrong. Disrespectful and a little ungrateful, talking about you like that in your own bed while you lay in the next room amongst the chaos of our possessions.

You told us you were better than you used to be. Though when you heard groups of people laughing in public places, you still believed it to be at your expense. Some things could not be helped, you said. Little things. But you were getting better. You told us this as we drank around your small table, late one hot night when nobody could sleep and wasps were dying all over your kitchen. There are progressive stills of your window sill, little yellow bodies lined up, gathering summer dust. We didn't know what was killing them but we weren't sorry to see them dead. We checked each empty glass before drinking from it, because they had a tendency to die in glassware. When we found one it would join the others on the sill. By the time we left the tally was in the low thirties.

That city was like a theatre set, or a lucid dream. We turned its corners too fast and there would be parts missing, as though we hadn't imagined it properly. Watch out for the drug dealers in Hasenheide Park, you told us, but all we saw was a woman walking like she was about to hit something, her body tensed up in a rage so complete it was almost majestic.

We spent so long in that place we began to speak in broken English. It's possible we did this unintentionally, in order to be more clearly understood by those who spoke it as a second language. One milk please, one bread. You began correcting us, saying that was not how English would break here, if it were to be broken. So we settled for speaking as formally as you did, with fewer contractions, no slang or colloquialisms. We drank in bars that ran out of the backs of bombed-out buildings or in bars where the furniture had been bolted to the ceiling upside-down, and dutifully we collected our hand portraits, favouring chipped fingernails, nicotine stains, scars, tattoos and varicose veins. There was a scar about an inch and a half long on the back of your left hand that we wouldn't leave alone.

I told you already. There was a trick with a knife I used to be able to do.

Yes, but can you show us this trick?

I am no longer able to do it properly. The scar is from the time after the last time the trick was done properly.

Was it the one where you stab the spaces between your fingers, getting faster and faster?

No, it was a different trick.

Sometimes you would come with us as an interpreter, approaching people in restaurants and at train stations. You explained our project while people looked past you suspiciously to where we stood with our old Leicas hanging from our necks. We didn't know the words for 'collective' and 'residual', but we knew that the word for guilt was *Schuld* and we never heard you use it in any of your explanations, so we knew you weren't saying the things we had told you to say. But almost everyone you spoke to would eventually shrug and nod, and you'd bring them over to us with that slow-moving smile, so we didn't care all that much about what you'd told them.

We kept a little notebook with entries for each pair of hands we photographed, listing names, ages and distinguishing characteristics so that we could match them up with corresponding photographs when the film was developed:

Lana. Fem. 23. Picture of Kafka's face tattooed inside right wrist.

Christoph. Male. 53. Tip of left index finger lost in factory accident.

Eva. Fem. Early 40s (?). Bright red fingernails filed to points. Plain gold wedding ring.

Sometimes we forgot the notebook, and other notes were written on small slips of paper and on the backs of receipts which were eventually lost between there and here.

After our film canisters have been cleared from your refrigerator, after your bed is your own bed again, we sit on a lounge-room floor on the other side of the world and hold negative strips up to the light. We can't remember the name of the kid with the bruised knuckles; the hairdresser whose fingers were stained purple with dye; which cafe we were in when we met the waitress with a reminder scrawled across the back of her left hand in blue pen, *Tiny Vipers – Schokoladen – Donnerstag.*

When we develop the photographs, moving around each other in the chemical dark of a room that was once a second bathroom, your scar from the trick with a knife is not among them. Just the mention of it in the diary, *Fynn. 37. Scar from a trick with a knife on back of left hand.* And a photograph of you standing by the Rosa Luxemburg memorial on the Landwehrkanal. Another and another of your kitchen window sill lined with the hateful dead insects. There's you wiping your hair out of your eyes, the desperate kindness creasing them at the corners, making us wary, and we have left all your letters unanswered.

Even so, our missing lens cap arrives one morning,

carefully swaddled in tissue and bubble-wrap and sent by registered post. The wasps are still dying, you write. There are now fifty-seven.

Sometimes beautiful, sometimes magical

If she had looked up she would have seen it, and it would have reminded her that the world was sometimes beautiful, sometimes magical. But she was standing at a window eleven storeys above Nueve de Julio, and nobody looks up from that height. She looked down into the street and saw the crawling traffic and knew it was loud down there but none of the loudness came into her room. In the room it was silent, and her skin still smelled of airline hand sanitiser. Feet still swollen inside her boots from the fourteen-hour flight. She waited for the city to show her something beautiful or magical, and when there wasn't anything she came away from the double-paned window and lay on the bed. The glass shading the ceiling light was a concave frosted dish. Through the frosted glass she could see all the black specks where insects had crawled in and died under the hot light.

St Leonards Avenue

Did you say that?

What, *Cheating bastard*, or *Let me the hell out the cab now and I hope you crash on the way home*?

Any of it.

Well, you know. I was feeling pretty bad. You know what Casualty is like on the weekend.

Yeah. Yeah I do.

So I called him a cheating bastard.

And you got out of the cab?

And I got out of the cab.

Tarcutta wake

These days I only ever see her at funerals. Which is more often than one might reasonably expect, our little set practically toppling in on top of one another before anyone's had a chance to unwrap the Merric Boyd pottery or to use the Old Holland oils and Escoda brushes willed to them by the most recently toppled. Laura, though: I believe she'll outlast everyone. She'll be there before the service, studying the photo board. Her fingers tracing the jawline and cheekbones in mid air, conjuring. Perhaps remembering her hand on their face.

A portrait artist with face blindness. *Prosopagnosia.* We thought she was joking. Then when we knew she wasn't joking, we thought her heart must be an empty room with a mud floor that anybody could walk through. We were wrong about that too. But she would sometimes mistake Ruth for me, foxed by the sharp elbows and wide Macedonian mouth, and by the loose-fitting shifts we both wore to hide our skinniness.

When Robin dies, it is my sister who drives me across the border, our funeral clothes lying flat across the back seat as she speeds past the water towers and granite war memorials of small country towns. World War II artillery mounted in front of public pools, tiny crooked cemeteries where we stop to stretch our legs, where sun has taken the colour out of everything. Fresh flowers on baby graves with headstones from 1958, 1974. Lived ten days, lived six days. The kind of loyalty to grief to which I could never relate. But I know that Ruth is thinking of Adeline – how can she not be? – of the jars of coffee and passata smashed against the bitumen, the trolley boys who came running. She was only thirty-three, the same age Ruth had been on the day she came running in from the pottery to throw up in the kitchen sink and reluctantly declare herself pregnant.

At Euroa I offer to drive, and Ruth laughs me off. Esther, she says. Dearheart. You know you can't. They took your licence away how long ago?

Ruth's left arm rests against the steering wheel in a blue Velcro brace. She got carpal tunnel towards the end of the '80s, and has worn the brace intermittently in the decades since. Mostly out of habit, if you ask me, though I'd never come right out and say so. At first we had all been a little bit jealous of the brace and what it stood for:

that Ruth had wrecked herself a fraction for the sake of her art. It made the rest of us feel like we weren't working hard enough. I secretly hoped to catch up with her, being three years younger, but it never came about. Dabbing a brush to a canvas yields different results from throwing clay at a wheel. In any case, the rest of us eventually weakened in our varied and less enviable fashions.

By the time we reach Holbrook it's nearing midday. Seventy kilometres until Tarcutta, and three hours until we need to be there. Ruth pulls into a motel and we pay for a twin room that smells of stale smoke and mouse shit, but she doesn't seem to notice. She sinks gratefully onto the bed farthest from the window.

Just a couple of hours here, Es. Then we'll be fresh for the wake.

Fresh for the wake. We shed our driving clothes in crumpled, sweaty heaps beside the twin beds. Ruth has already taken off her brace and nestled it beside her pillow. She looks more vulnerable without it, the skin of her left arm a pale sleeve. She curls up to face the wall, and her spine showing through her white slip reminds me of the skeletons of swans, their rickety necks bereft of muscle and feather.

This is how I've come to measure my own fragility. There was a time when I believed Ruth to be ageing independently of me; that I was somehow fixed in place, standing on the dock waving while she drifted off towards some bleak horizon. Now I know better.

I watch her sleep: one of Edward Hopper's girls that nobody ever came for.

From the motel window I can see the hull of the decommissioned submarine looming over the park, schoolchildren clambering over it like yellow ticks on a dead black beast. I once watched this same sub dive and surface in Sydney Harbour before a crowd of onlookers. Ruth had been standing next to me, holding on to Adeline's little hand. I have seen the rise and fall of so many things.

Time is not the longest distance, despite what Tennessee Williams said. It is a room you can step into and out of at will, though you cannot pick anything up, cannot rearrange things the way you'd like to. Though sometimes you'll return to it to find that someone else has done it for you: taken things away, locked drawers. It is a room where the titles have been wiped from the spines of all the books and the windows are nailed shut.

Ruth wakes with a sharp inhale a little after one-thirty. I hear her turn over.

Esther? Bella, you didn't snooze. What are you looking at out there?

Nothing, really. Schoolkids.

You're worried about Laura.

Not worried, exactly.

Ruth stifles a yawn. Okay, she says. But if you're not ready to speak to her yet, just affect a limp or something. She's like a Tyrannosaurus Rex.

A what?

You know, she scoffs. Motion sensors. She'll know you're you just by the way you move.

Laura has developed a number of methods for recognising people. She'll wait for them to speak first. She'll memorise wedding rings, laughter, the shape of their eyebrows. Tattoos and scars are a blessing. When Nola got the mole above her top lip removed, Laura was crestfallen, because without it Nola was a blank page. She told me all of this matter-of-factly, priming a canvas in the studio of the Artists' Society. It was like being savvy to a magician's tricks, and I watched her from then on. I saw the little light that flickered on when she recognised a voice or a bit of jewellery. I asked her how she knew that I was me. *By the way you move, E. It's like your feet never touch the ground.* I'd be lying if I said that wasn't what started it.

I know you blame me, Es. But she knew what she was doing. Maybe it began as a mistake, but she knew.

I know that, Ruth.

And I know I should be sorry. And I am sorry that it hurt you. But even so, it was something I carried around with me. Something folded small that I could take out and look at whenever I wanted to. And you know how it was, in those days, Es. No one really belonged to anyone . . . Es?

All afternoon the sky has threatened rain, despite the heat. There is the kind of tension that will only be eased by some manner of violence. A pin tapped through the blackened nail of a hammer-cracked thumb.

We should get going, I say to Ruth. Come on, before it rains.

Nobody understands why Robin wanted his ashes scattered over that muddy little trickle in Tarcutta. And when we meet his sister in the front bar of the hotel, she just shrugs. Robin's three teenage daughters, all long-limbed and nervous as horses, hiding their eyes behind their dark manes: they do not know either. They sit together, elbows on the same sticky table, sipping at glasses of post-mix cola and red creaming soda. The eldest flicks her eyes up at me, tries for a weak smile, but the other two are staring at the space between their glasses and the earthenware jar on the table. If Ruth is pleased about the choice of container, she doesn't give any indication. Perhaps it's too early a work, too clumsy to lay claim to. But I don't need to run my fingers along the underneath to know her mark is there.

I never even heard him talk about Tarcutta, his sister is saying. I thought he would have wanted to be with Leonie, but it was right there in the will. He called me a few months back to make sure he had my address right. He said, You're the executor, okay? I said, Okay. But he never said anything about Tarcutta.

I see Robin, the reminders scrawled on his hands and wrists for the last ten years of his life. *Call Susannah.*

Slowly filling in the documents, the careful block letters he would use to spell his sister's name. He rarely spoke about death or sickness or the fear of either, but his work gravitated away from the familiar watercolour landscapes and portraits to portrayals of mortality: boarded-up houses, broken timepieces, a skulk of shot foxes strung along a wire fence.

When a humpback whale washed up dead on Sandon Point, he drove there as soon as he heard to spend the afternoon sketching the decomposing beast, the ventral grooves like the ridges and furrows in a white field, the barnacles encircling the shut-tight eye, the massive penis hanging limp across the bloated belly.

It's all a bit morbid, Rob, I told him over the phone when the photographs arrived. Not something I'd have on my wall.

I heard him laugh down the line. We were as unforgiving of wall-destined art as we were of photorealism: *Isn't that nice, dear? It looks just like the thing it's supposed to look like.*

To hell with it, I said. These are the lemon peel years, after all. You may as well call a spade a spade.

There is no photo board at the Horse and Jockey, no reminders of what Robin or anybody else looks like or used to look like – little help to Laura, who sweeps the room with the same vague smile she uses everywhere, a look that hovers between recognition and introduction. Enough to make one believe they haven't been forgotten. Not so much as to unsettle anyone she hasn't actually met. Searchlighting, I used to call it.

She sees me standing there with Ruth, and the light goes on but I don't know who it's for. I watch her drift towards our table, and I think of all the things it's too late to understand. Beneath her grey silk dress I know her body is as soft as old money, as over-handled paper. *Something folded small.*

Esther, she finally says. Let me look at you, she says, and brings her hands up to my face. I let her look, without knowing what she is looking for.

You've hardly changed, she says, but she'd hardly know. A ridiculous longing growls through my bones. For all of us, for what we all were and didn't become. And when did longing move from my belly to my bones. When did that happen.

We gather outside the pub, Susannah holding the earthenware jar that is holding Robin. The sound of the trucks pulling into the service station next door is like whale song. The sky has held. Nobody has thought to cry yet.

Okay, Susannah says. She puts her hands on the youngest daughter's bony shoulders. Let's do this.

We walk single or double file along the side of the highway until finally we stand by the pitiful creek, eleven of us, our good shoes sinking into the soft mud. Susannah takes the cork lid from the jar. She dips her slender hand inside to scoop up a handful of Robin's ashes.

I remember when we were little, she says. About ten and twelve. That Christmas he gave me my present all wrapped up in red tissue paper and silk ribbon. He'd taken so much care. When I opened it there was just a rock. Not quartz or anything special. It wasn't shaped like a duck or a woman's face or what-have-you. It was just an ordinary little rock. He thought it was so funny, nearly killed himself laughing, and Dad made him sit on the back step until lunch was called. Next Christmas, I gave it back to him, wrapped even more beautifully. And he gave it back the year after, in a little wooden box Joe helped him carve. It went on like that for years, until I can't remember when. But when we were clearing up his things last week, there it was. He'd been holding onto it all that time.

She opens her hand over the water, and the rock drops into the creek with a gentle plip amid the shower of ashes.

I expect the girls to baulk at this, but they pass the jar between them, each reaching in for a handful of their father's ashes. They stand at the creek side, eldest to youngest:

I remember when he had to quit drinking, he went through his collecting phase. Some people just eat more when they stop drinking, but he collected things. So every week we'd be dragged along to a Sunday trash-and-treasure, helping him dig around for paper moon portraits or cigarette tins or whatever. Always small things, and they got smaller and smaller, until it was matchbooks. Matchbooks. At some market, I don't remember where, he finds this matchbook from the '60s, from some pub in Melbourne he used to drink at. And he says, look at this, girls, it's still got matches in it. And we say, great. Mission accomplished. And the guy says, eighty bucks. Dad's still holding onto it, thinking about paying eighty bucks for six matches, and Michelle just looks at him. She didn't say anything, just gave him this look like, Dad, are you mental? And he puts them down and that's the end of the matchbooks. He just kind of got on with it after that.

I remember when Johanna was thrown from that horse. When Dad carried her in from the paddock I watched him climbing the front steps with Jo in his arms and I thought. God, I thought. She was really busted up, you know. And by then I'd started thinking that Dad was a bit useless, always forgetting things, sometimes really important things. But right then he just looked like some kind of hero.

Oh, that was going to be mine. Okay, I remember after the horse. After Molly threw me off I was afraid to get back on. I was afraid of all horses but horses were the only thing I was good at. So I was bored and sad and then Dad said, Why don't you try drawing them instead? Before that I knew words like withers and chestnut and fetlock, but I didn't know throatlatch or gaskin or stifle. I hadn't looked closely enough. I know now that's what he was getting me to do, to look closer. Cause you're not so afraid of things when you can see them properly.

Johanna steps forward, creek water spilling into her sandals. She bends low so that her face is close to the water, and says something beyond the reach of human hearing. Then she dips her cupped hand into the stream like she's letting go of a delicate creature.

When they pass the jar to me, I remember nothing. I remember everything at once, all the edges of our years together overlapping, and no way to lift a corner of any single instance. Robin's ashes have the weight of sand and I cannot remember his face, but places I've not seen in thirty years rise up like the heat shimmering off the rooftops of cars parked along a coastal road, all the shops closed as though it's Christmas Day – perhaps it is. But there are card games that we played on the day the bridge collapsed, the phone call to say that Whitlam was out or that *Poor Fellow* had won, though we were, at the same time, very drunk, very young, carousing in the corner at that Blackman exhibition, and Robin running into the roiling green ocean and running into the roiling green ocean and running uneasy and beautiful and not turning around. *Like something folded small. I carried it around with me.* Well, yes, I could take it out and look at it again and again.

I remember how he laughed when he met me. I asked what was funny and he said he'd tell me one day. He never did.

★

Ruth slumps into the passenger seat, graceless with exhaustion. She waves a bird-boned hand at me. 'Go on and drive then, Es. But it'll be your fine if they stop us.'

Further down the Hume I speed up to overtake a white station wagon, and we are flying then, down the right-hand lane. This is perhaps how it happens: something crashing through the line of trees, a roo or a loose horse, my sister asleep at my shoulder. There are worse ways.

Outside the windows the world has grown bleary. A confusion of native and European trees borders the highway, and beyond that the paddocks are a thin wash of grey-green. Poor man's colours, I decide. Beautiful all the same, like the grey that Gamblin makes from all the leftover pigment and gives away each April. Scraped-up flakes of all the other colours mixed together, so that it's different every year; some years more blue, some years more green, though you can't tell without comparing them side by side – this year and last year and the year before. How little it takes to be changed, and how difficult to know of it. How little we can see, even from here.

Acknowledgments

My sincere thanks to John Hunter, for his ongoing encouragement, and for lighting a spark under this collection. Thank you to Madonna Duffy and Rebecca Roberts, and to UQP, for continuing to champion short stories.

Thank you, Christopher Merrill, the University of Iowa, and all the staff and writers involved in the 2011 International Writing Program: it was a surreal and enriching experience. Thank you, Gabrielle Connellan and the US Consulate General for all your help on this side of the equator.

Thank you, Chris Flynn, John Skibinski, and Boyacks for years of friendship, love and support (editorial, familial and illustrative).

Thank you, Patrick Pittman, for everything.

I am deeply grateful to the following publications for their support, and to those editors who worked closely with me to refine earlier versions. I would especially like to thank Melissa Cranenburgh from *The Big Issue* and David Winter from *Griffith Review* for their time and expertise.

'Suitable for a lampshade' in *Australian Book Review* and *Award Winning Australian Writing* (Melbourne Books, 2011).

'Brisbane' in *Small Room* and *The Best Australian Stories 2010* (Black Inc., 2010), edited by Cate Kennedy.

'In the mornings we would sometimes hear him singing' and 'View' in *The Big Issue*.

'Repairs' in *Escape: An anthology of short stories* (Spineless Wonders, 2011), edited by Bronwyn Mehan.

'The tank' in *Griffith Review*.

'Dixieland', 'The taxidermist's wife' and 'Vending machine at the end of the world' in *The Iowa Review*.

'Hotels' in *Meanjin*.

'Scar from a trick with a knife' in *Wet Ink*.

In 'The tank', the line 'Let everything happen to you: beauty and terror' is taken from Rainer Maria Rilke's poem 'God speaks'.

In 'Raising the wreck', the line 'the thing itself, and not the myth' is taken from the Adrienne Rich poem 'Diving into the wreck'.

Add to your collection with UQP's short fiction series

THE REST IS WEIGHT

Jennifer Mills

'A writer of extraordinary range and imagination'
Cate Kennedy

A girl searches for her lost grandmother while her parents quarrel at home. A young architect finds herself entangled by a strange commission. A man contemplates inertia after toxic fallout changes life in a remote Australian town. A woman imagines a mother's love for her autistic son.

The award-winning stories in *The Rest is Weight* Mills reflect Jennifer Mills' years in Central Australia, as well as her travels to Mexico, Russia and China. Sometimes dreamy and hypnotic, sometimes dark, comic and wry, Mills weaves themes of longing, alienation, delusion, resilience, and love. Collected or on their own, these stories are both a joy and a wonder to read.

'Shifting effortlessly from the naturalistic to the deeply surreal, these stories conjure a whole sensory universe and the exiles who inhabit it with images that lodge in your head and just won't leave. Mills' precision is breathtaking.' *Cate Kennedy*

PRAISE FOR JENNIFER MILLS

'Clearly a talent' *Australian Book Review*
'Highly original' *Sydney Morning Herald*
'Brilliant' *Bookseller + Publisher*

ISBN 978 0 7022 4940 2

More *brilliant* fiction from UQP

BLOOD

Tony Birch

Shortlisted for the 2012 Miles Franklin Literary Award

Jesse has sworn to protect his sister, Rachel, no matter what. It's a promise that cannot be broken. A promise made in blood. But, when it comes down to life or death, how can he find the courage to keep it?

Set on the back roads of Australia, *Blood* is a boy's odyssey through a broken-down adult world.

'Irresistibly compelling.' *Sydney Morning Herald*

'Nothing short of outstanding. Tony Birch could take home a few prizes, deservedly so. *Blood* is a humanist masterpiece that has been worth the wait.' *Australian Book Review*

'*Blood* keeps us on edge from the outset. Jesse is an endearing mix of love, cynicism, patience and survival instincts.' *Good Reading*

'A novel about what makes and what breaks a family. It is emotional. It is at turns tender and intense. It is a novel worth reading.' *Avid Reader*

'Darkly suffused with the gritty realism of young children doing it tough in a world of dysfunctional adults' *Sunday Canberra Times*

'An absorbing and endearing tale of children in adversity. The story is told from Jesse's point of view, and Birch pulls this off beautifully with a compelling combination of flinty Australian vernacular and boyish candour. It's impressive stuff.' *Weekend Australian*

ISBN 978 0 7022 4954 9

UQP

THE ANATOMY OF WINGS

Karen Foxlee

**Winner 2008 Commonwealth Writers' Prize –
Best First Book South East Asia and Pacific Region
Winner of the Dobbie Award
Shortlisted for the Barbara Jefferis Award**

Ten-year-old Jennifer Day lives in a small mining town full of secrets. Trying to make sense of the sudden death of her teenage sister Beth, she looks to the adult world around her for answers.

As she recounts the final months of Beth's life, Jennifer sifts through the lies and the truth, but what she finds are mysteries, miracles and more questions. Was Beth's death an accident? Why couldn't Jennifer – or anyone else – save her?

Through Jennifer's eyes, we see one girl's failure to cross the threshold into adulthood. We see a family slowly falling apart. In this award-winning novel, Karen Foxlee captures perfectly the essence of growing up in a small town and the complexities and absurdities of family life.

'An exceptional novel' *Sydney Morning Herald*

'The metaphors embedded in the story and the luscious prose will hold readers until the moving conclusion.' *Publishers Weekly*

ISBN 978 0 7022 3698 3